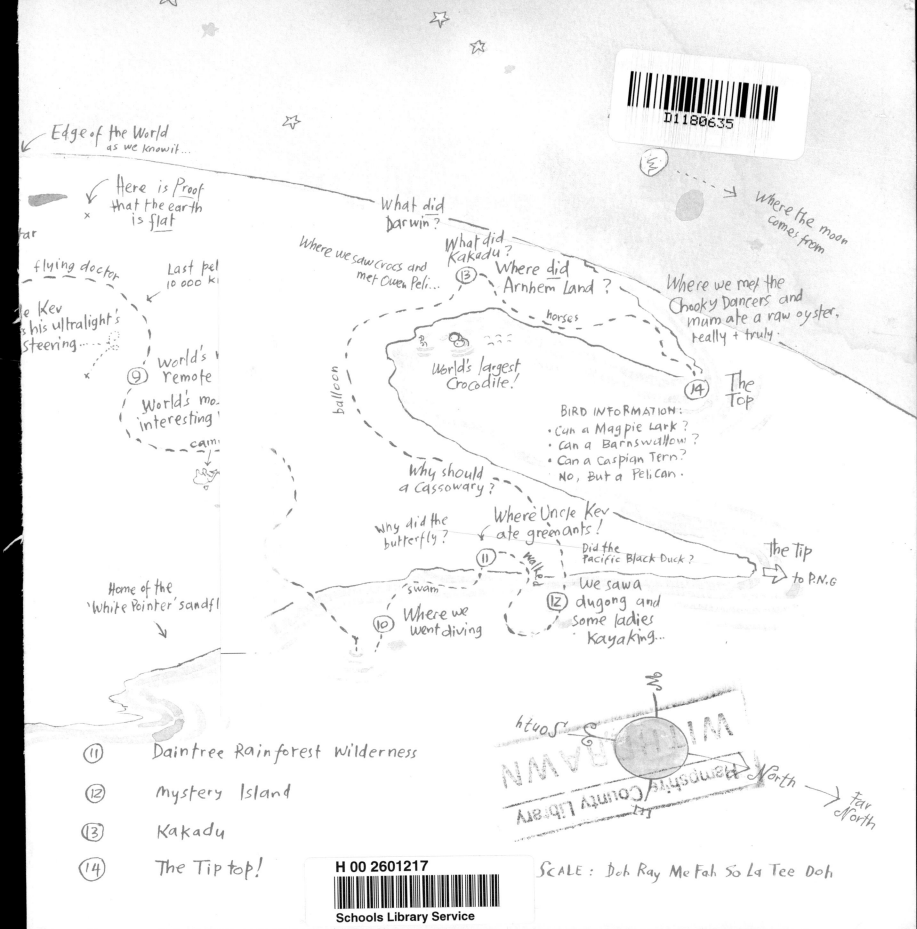

Edge of the World *as we know it...*

Here is Proof that the earth is flat
×

Where the moon comes from

What did Darwin?

Where we saw crocs and met Owen Peli...

What did Kakadu?

⑬

Where did Arnhem Land?

horses

Where we met the Chooky Dancers and mum ate a raw oyster, really + truly.

⑭ The Top

flying doctor

Last pel 10 000 k

World's largest Crocodile!

Kev his ultralight's steering.....

balloon

BIRD INFORMATION:
• Can a Magpie Lark?
• Can a Barnswallow?
• Can a Caspian Tern?
• No, But a Pelican.

⑨ World's remote

World's mo. interesting

cam

Why should a Cassowary?

Where Uncle Kev ate green ants!

Why did the butterfly?

the Tip ⇨ to P.N.G

Did the Pacific Black Duck?

walked

Home of the 'White Pointer' sandfl

swam

⑩ Where we went diving

⑪

⑫ We saw a dugong and some ladies kayaking...

⑪ Daintree Rainforest Wilderness

⑫ Mystery Island

⑬ Kakadu

⑭ The Tip top!

SCALE: Doh Ray Me Fah So La Tee Doh

To the TOP END

Our trip across Australia

Roland Harvey

ALLEN&UNWIN

In the Wilderness, Uncle Kevin used his Commando training to take some people white-water rafting...

He said that here in the rainforest there are wombats...

Dad showed us the safe way to cross a log bridge...

Some trees are so tall they could touch the clouds...

...rosellas

...Tassie Devils...

...but...

and no Thylacines...

... and Frankie spotted fish.

In Bass Strait it was very rough and very windy... and Penny spent a lot of time feeding the

we saw dolphins and boats

we saw socks and undies

and diving birds

and we saw seals

and we would have seen sharks except they're scared of Uncle Kev...

and giant squid

fish and a dolphin stole our red ball and

Uncle Kev told us about giant sea creatures and it was SCARY.

But we don't believe him...

do we...

Dolphins swam around our boat...

We saw a blue whale called 'Humpty' who had a calf

which we haven't named yet...

Uncle Kev told stories of giant creatures living in the depths, but they're not true

Bogong Jack's Hut is the noisiest place on the High Plains.

whisper
whisper

creak...
Creak...

skreearchhh...

rustle
rustle

aaarr...

In a deep dark damp gully a lyrebird sang a hundred songs of different birds

Sigh

roarrr...

whinny

oooh!

rroarrr

neigh

oooh!

Croak
Croak

sploosh

plop

ssssshhh

swoosh

scrape

screech

Kaaaarrr...
aaaaarrr...r

thump

zzzzzzzz

rusty hinge
rusty hinge...

chirp
chirp
warble
warble

and on a distant mountainside, another answered...

...r whit

mmmphh

gurgle

bok bok bok
bok bok

Peeee...

ts.ts.ts..

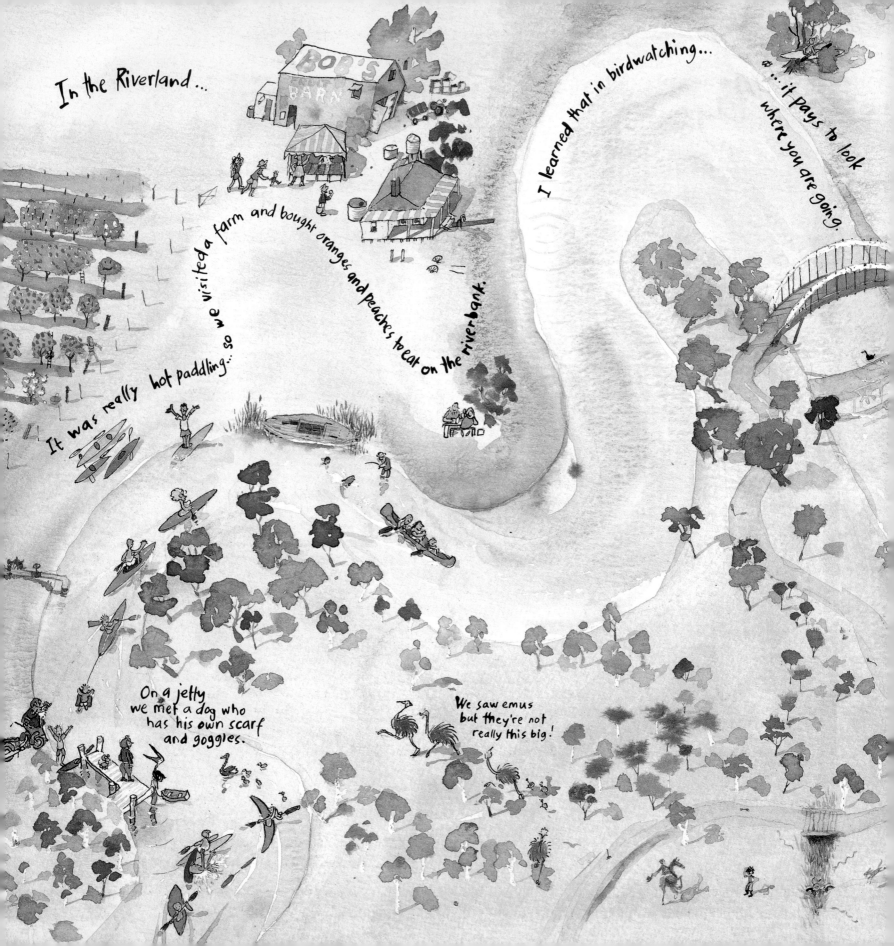

In the Riverland...

BOB'S FRUIT BARN

It was really hot paddling... so we visited a farm and bought oranges and peaches to eat on the river bank.

I learned that in birdwatching... ...it pays to look where you are going.

On a jetty we met a dog who has his own scarf and goggles.

We saw emus but they're not really this big!

At Kata Tjuta, Uncle Kev went for

We played

and

seek

hide

Henry has such an imagination! He thinks one rock looks like Uncle Kev, only smaller.

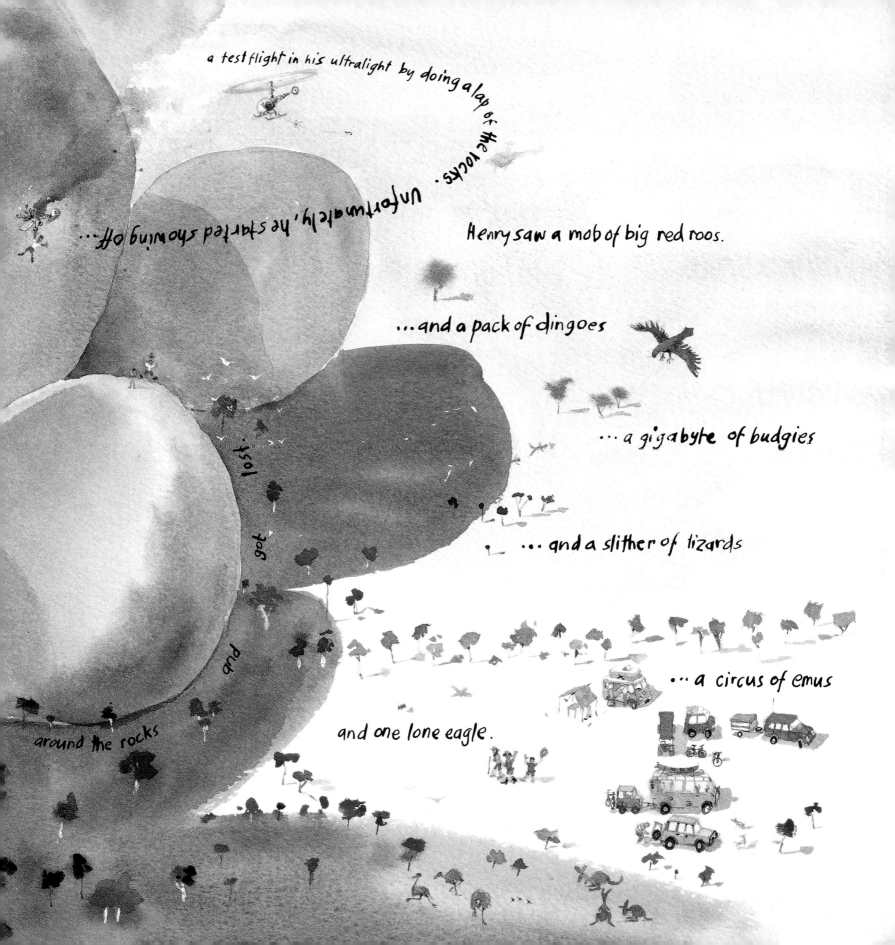

a test flight in his ultralight by doing a lap of the rocks. Unfortunately, he started showing off...

...to buimoys pəʇɹɐʇs əɥ 'ʎləʇɐunʇɹoɟun

Henry saw a mob of big red roos.

...and a pack of dingoes

...a gigabyte of budgies

...and a slither of lizards

...a circus of emus

around the rocks

and

got

lost.

and one lone eagle.

A soaring wedgetail watched us all   from high above the cliffs

...I think...

I didn't want to dance in front
of my family. I went off to look for
water monsters, but they're just a myth...

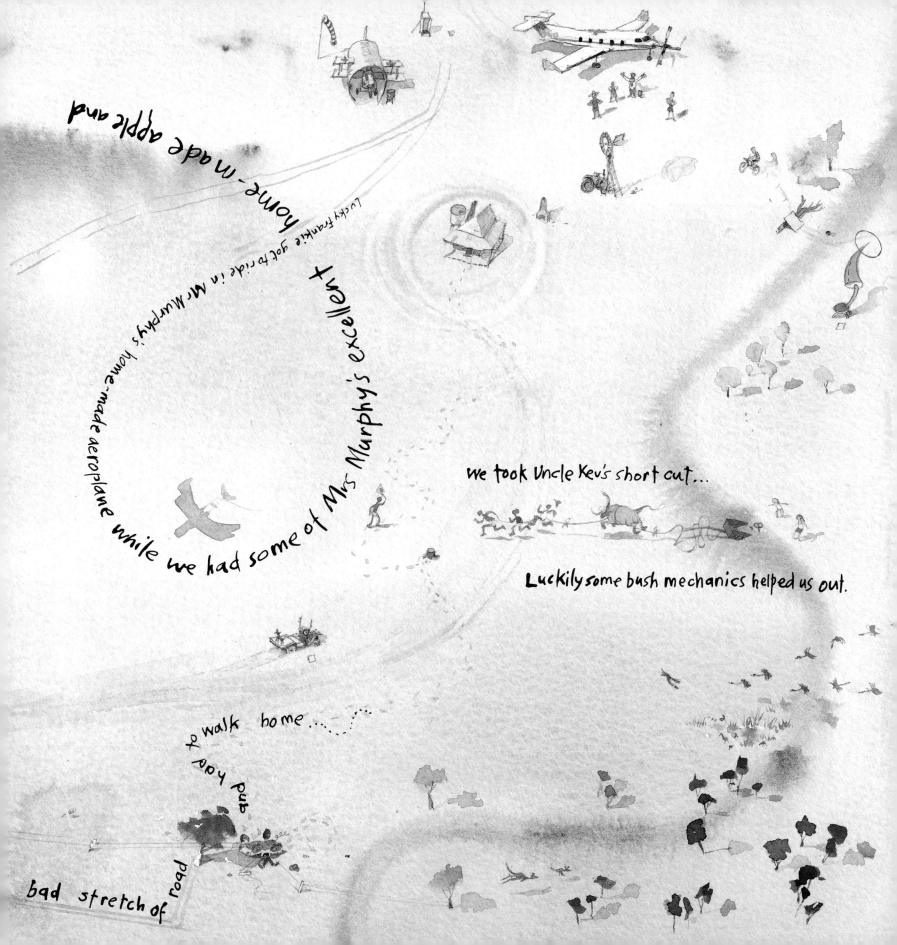

home-made apple and home-made aeroplane while we had some of Mrs Murphy's excellent

Luckily Frankie got a ride in Mr Murphy's

We took Uncle Kev's short cut...

Luckily some bush mechanics helped us out.

had to walk home......

bad stretch of road

pub

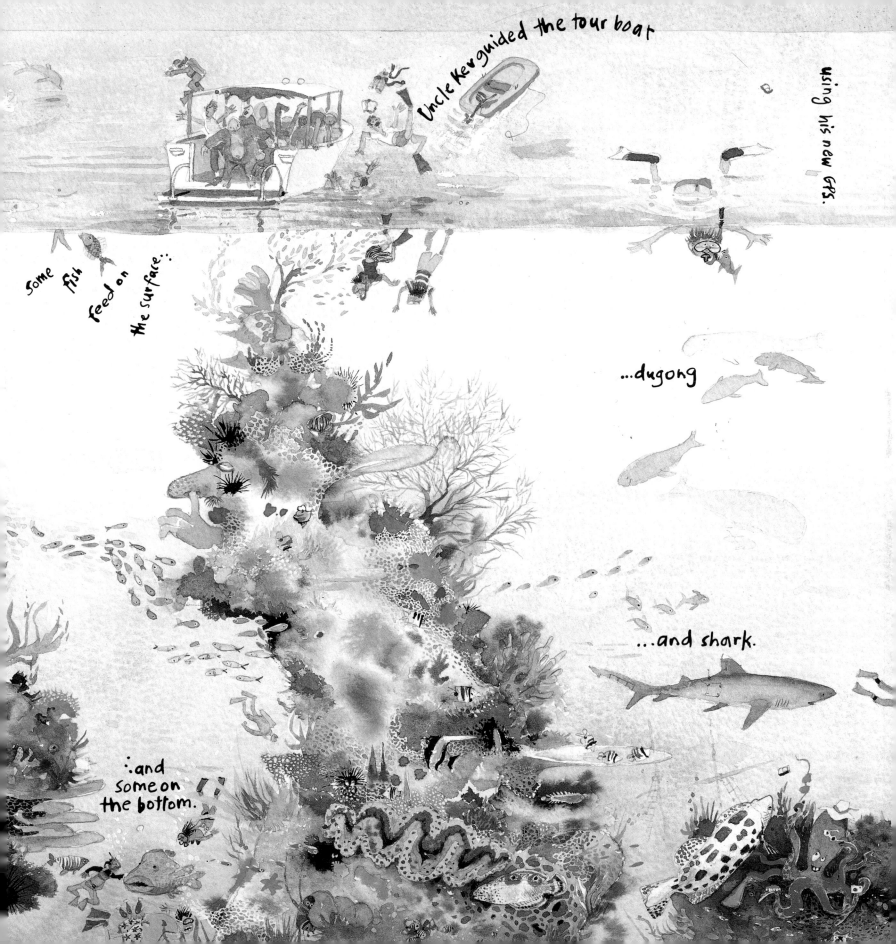

Uncle Kev guided the tour boat using his new GPS.

Some fish feed on the surface∴

∴and some on the bottom.

...dugong

...and shark.

Deep in the Daintree Rainforest Wilderness...

Turquoise

Swallowtailed

butterflies

A dragon scurried up a tree...

...and a butterfly

alighted on a vine.

Uncle Kev ate Green Ants!

flickered

about...

A brilliant Azure Kingfisher swooped low over the water...

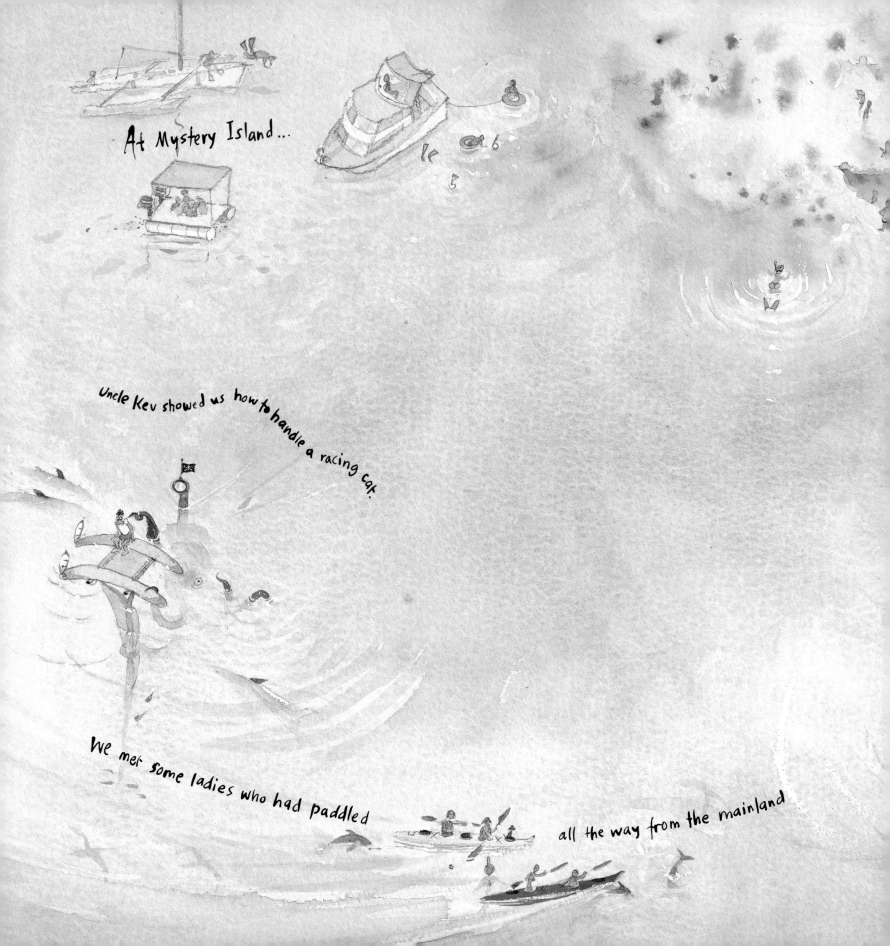

At Mystery Island...

Uncle Kev showed us how to handle a racing cat.

We met some ladies who had paddled all the way from the mainland

A pod of dolphins played around the ferry.

People came from town to enjoy the solitude...

We fed fish

...and snorkelled around the reef...

and sat on the pure white sand.

to stay on the island.

Visiting boats anchor in the deeper water...

5:30 AM at Yellow Water and it is already hot.
We had a bird-spotting competition.
I saw 5 million birds, but
Frankie won with 32 billion.

We saw ducks fishing

and fish ducking

and waterlilies

and an eagle.

We saw turtles and Salties and magpie geese and spoonbills...
...and a jabiru and brolgas and egrets and some Americans.

YAY! We made it from Tassie to the very tip of the TOP End . . .

and it floated back to me !

I kicked the ball to a brolga and she headed it to an emu but a kangaroo hit it to a turtle and she swam it out to a shark and he gave it to some dolphins and they passed it up to my uncle . . . and he kicked it right out of Australia . . . .

Then we all sat down and had a campfire feast.

WISH YOU WERE HERE!

 The Wilds of Tasmania

 Sailing the high seas of lower Bass Strait

The High Country

 The Murray River

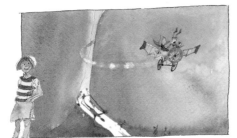 Wallaby-spotting in the Flinders Ranges

 Down-Under Coober Pedy

 Picnic at Kata Tjuta

 The Gorge

 The Great Thirsty Desert

 The Great Big Barrier Reef

Deep in the Daintree

 Mystery Island

 Crocs of Kakadu

 Near the Tip of the Top End

To Bob and Carol

First published in 2009

Allen & Unwin
83 Alexander St
Crows Nest NSW 2065
Australia
Phone: (61 2) 8425 0100
Fax: (61 2) 9906 2218
Email: info@allenandunwin.com
Web: www.allenandunwin.com

National Library of Australia
Cataloguing-in-Publication entry:

Harvey, Roland, 1945–.
To the top end: our trip across Australia/ Roland Harvey.

ISBN 978 1 74175 884 9 (hbk.)

1: Australia – Description and travel – Juvenile fiction.

A823.3

Illustration technique: dip pen and watercolour
Designed by Roland Harvey and Sandra Nobes
This book was printed in April 2010 at Tien Wah Press (PTE) Limited,
4 Pandan Crescent, Singapore 128475

3 5 7 9 10 8 6 4 2

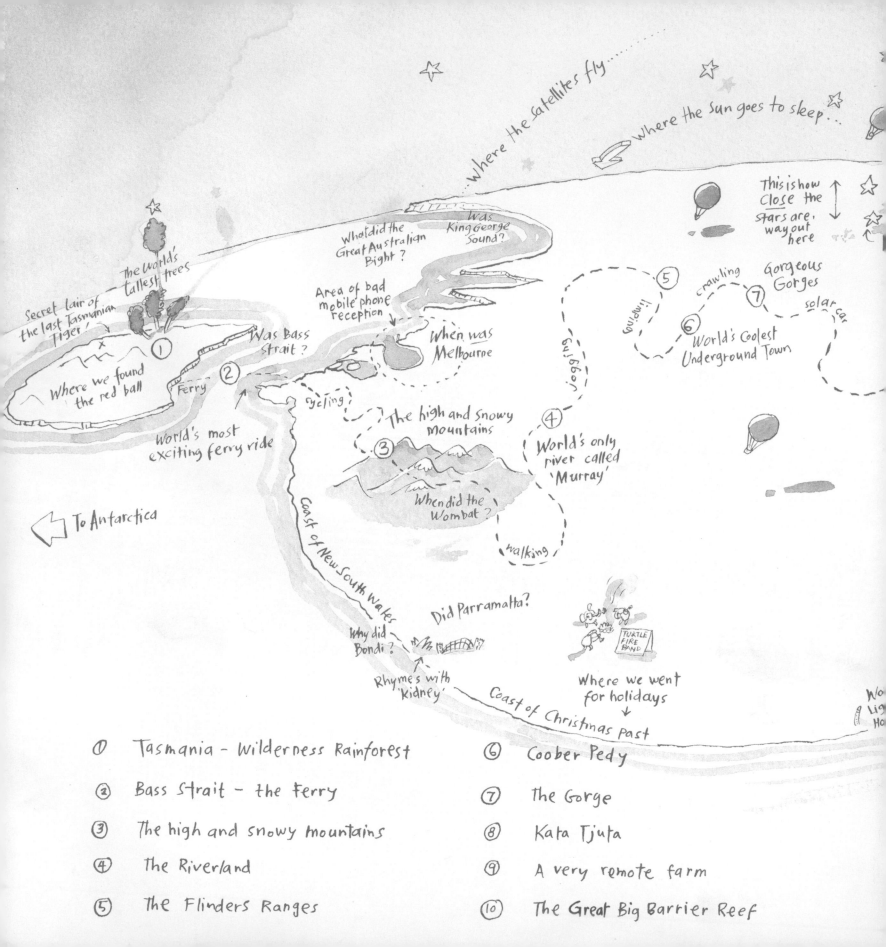

Where the satellites fly.......

Where the sun goes to sleep...

This is how close the stars are, way out here

The World's tallest trees

Secret lair of the last Tasmanian Tiger!

Where we found the red ball

Was Bass Strait?

Ferry

① ②

World's most exciting ferry ride

To Antarctica

What did the Great Australian Bight?

Was King George Sound?

Area of bad mobile phone reception

When was Melbourne

cycling

The high and snowy Mountains

③

Coast of New South Wales

jogging

④ World's only river called 'Murray'

When did the Wombat?

walking

crawling

Gorgeous Gorges

⑤

⑥ World's Coolest Underground Town

⑦

solar car

Did Parramatta?

Why did Bondi?

Rhymes with 'kidney'

Coast of Christmas Past

TURTLE FIRE BAND

Where we went for holidays

Wo Lig Ho

① Tasmania - Wilderness Rainforest

② Bass Strait - the Ferry

③ The high and snowy mountains

④ The Riverland

⑤ The Flinders Ranges

⑥ Coober Pedy

⑦ The Gorge

⑧ Kata Tjuta

⑨ A very remote farm

⑩ The Great Big Barrier Reef